WEREWOLF BY NIGHT

Werewolf By Night

Olivia Shread

Zombel Publishing

This book would not be possible without the loving support of my family. My Dad pushed me to make sure I finished this book you have here in your hands. My Mom helped me by editing the book and helping me make the cover art.

"Finish what you started."
- Russell James, Author of Devil In The Desert

1

"Hey Zach, I can't wait for your thirteenth birthday tonight." Amy said with anticipation.

"Yeah sis, I can't wait either", I said smiling. "It's going to be awesome!"

"Line up!", called the teacher.

"Aw man recess is over", said Amy.

"Stop whining sis, we're going to be late for pick up."

"Alright, alright, all right. I'm coming"

"Could you get any slower."

"Jeez, could you stop being so mean?"

"Ok we're here. You can stop running now, seriously you can stop running."

"I am just getting exercise."

"Please just sit down."

"Fine!"

"Hey, do you know where mom is?" I said

"She's right there."

"Where?"

"Approaching the roundabout."

"Zach, Amy, come on time to go home."

"Ok" Amy said.

"Coming" I said, while shutting the car door.

"So how was your day at school?"

"Meah" I said

"Good." said Mom. "So Amy, how was your day?"

"Awesome!"

"We had art, science and P.E. and... um... lots more!"

"What about you Zach?", Mom asked. "Did you have science, P.E. or art?"

"Zach, you there buddy?"

"Umuh.", I replied.

"What's Zach doing back there, Amy?"

"I hear people talking that are not in the car."

"Is he playing video games?", Mom asked.

"Yes he is on his phone.", Amy snitched.

"Zach! Give me the phone", Mom commanded.

"Why?"

"Because I said so.... Zach, the phone please."

"Uuuug", I protested.

"Now!", Mom demanded.

"Fine." Plop. I handed my mom the phone.

"Ha!" Amy said. "Girl power, right Mom?"

"Yep, sure is girl power."

"When can I have the phone back?" I pleaded.

"When you earn it" Mom said.

"I mean a date not 'when you earn it'. That's not a date" I complained.

"Well then I don't know. Alright, maybe by tomorrow morning."

"Great, that's a good answer."

"I know that is a great answer."

"Ugg", I moaned

"Yay!" Amy cheered. "We're home"

"So glad I don't have homework." I said with relief.

"Why do you say that?", Amy asked.

"Because I intend to play video games."

"But mom took away your phone!"

"The Xbox.", I confided.

"I took that away as well.", Mom said with a grin. "All right time to get out. Zach you can go take a nap."

"What! Why?"

"Because of all the sass you gave me in the car," Mom replied.

"Fine!" I said, slamming the car door behind me.

2

It was early morning about 7:00, maybe a little past. Amy and I just got up. We were very excited for my party because the whole family was going to be there. We barely get to see them.

"Zach! Amy! Get ready! The family is going to be here very soon", Mom shouted out.

"Ok." I said. I quickly got to work getting ready for the day. The party was going to be great!

Ding-dong!

"Zach! Amy! It's time for the party. Everyone is here!" Mom said.

"Coming!" Amy said.

"Zach don't come down or else you'll see the cake. It's a surprise", Mom told me.

"Got it".

I slowly walked to the wingback chair to sit down. It had a small pillow on it from Lilly Pulitzer, my mom's favorite.

"Huuu" I sighed.

"Alright you can come down now Zach!"

Thump, thump, thump. I ran down the stairs as fast as I could. Once I got to the bottom of the stairs, I looked at the floor so I couldn't see the cake and then sat in a chair at the head of the table. It looked like it was decorated for a king with balloons, streamers, and a banner above the chair that read "HAPPY BIRTHDAY ZACH!".

"Zach, get ready!" Mom yelled from the kitchen.

Then I heard faint whispers coming from the kitchen. I think they were saying 1, 2, 3 and to my surprise, after they all said three, they began singing.

When I saw the cake, I could have dropped dead from the look of it.

It had a werewolf baring its teeth with blood dripping down around the creature and from its mouth. The teeth were like freshly sharpened knives ready to rend its next prey. It had tangled and ragged fur dyed dark red from the blood of its victims. Its face was battle scarred and it had bloodshot eyes that never seemed to stop staring directly through my soul. But despite all that I still loved it!

Once they were done singing it was time to cut the cake. Of course I got the first piece of cake. Amy had to make an entire discussion about who should get the first piece. That took up most of my time. After we had the cake, I got to open up my presents. I got a Halloween Roblox edition with Werewolves, a 3 in 1 LEGO set which was awesome. And the best thing of all was when I got a Nintendo Switch from my grandma. I know I got a lot more but I can't remember.

Later at night we all crowded on the couch in the family room to watch a movie. I got to choose. We watched the movie Terminator. It was great!

When the movie was done, I heard a strange sound coming from outside. My mom and Amy heard it too. At first, we thought it was an animal, but the second time we heard it we decided to see what it was coming from. We were afraid that something bad had happened.

<h1 style="text-align:center">3</h1>

Amy, my mom and I went to investigate the noise.
"Amy, do you know what that sound is coming from?", I asked.

"No, do you?"

"Not a clue. What about you mom?" I asked.

"I don't know but I hope it's not something urgent"

"Like what?"

"Like a power line fell down or there's a bear outside like that sort of urgent"

Click. Mom unlocked the door and we all stepped out at once to figure out where that sound was coming from.

"Amy, Zach you two look to the left of the house I'll look to the right, got it?"

"Yep," Amy said.

Amy and I started walking to the left side of the house then we heard Mom calling out to us saying not to go too far away.

"Do you know what the rest of the family is doing inside?" I asked.

"I think they are playing a board game or something."

"Oh, by the way the cake was awesome!"

"I know, it tasted really good too", Amy smiled.

"Do you hear that?" I asked

"Yeah. Do you know what it is coming from?"

"No"

"I don't think we should go near it."

"Oh, don't be such a wimp", I teased. "It's probably just the wind or an animal."

"Yeah, a rabid animal."

"Hurry up, slow poke!"

"Fine!", Amy retorted. "Oh wow it's really foggy back here."

"I know. Oh and watch your step. I tripped on a tree root back there."

"Did you see that?" Amy asked, frightened to her wit's end.

"Yes."

"Ok! I had enough fun for tonight. Bye!" Amy said, running away crashing through the tree branches along the way.

"Amy! Amy! Don't leave me here all alone. Amy?!", I said in a whisper.

I felt a cold breeze hit the back of my neck. Then I felt something cold and sharp touch my shoulder. I slowly turned around to see what terror might be behind me. It was black, furry and had a long snout covered in scars. It was about 7 feet tall and looked almost human. This was the thing of my nightmares. I ran as fast as I could through the bushes and shrubs. I got scrapes all over my face and body. I never turned back until I got into the house.

"Hey Zach are you ok? We've been waiting for you." Amy said.

"I'm... I'm fine."

"Are you sure you're ok? You're all scratched up."

"No...I'm fine...all good.", I panted.

"Ok."

"Hey, is mom still out there?" I asked, trying not to sound scared

"No, she's back in the house. She is here wondering where you are. We should probably go tell her you're here."

Amy pranced happily down the hall then shouted back, "Are you coming?"

I took one last look outside to see if the thing was still there but all I could see was fog.

4

It was the next day when Mom finally noticed my scratches. She was really mad at me for not telling her last night. She said that because it was the day after my birthday she wouldn't ground me for the rest of the day. I was so glad she let me off the hook because I did not want to lose an entire day of my summer vacation. Now that would be horrible!

Last night I heard strange sounds coming from outside of my window. I know that Amy had heard it too because at breakfast this morning she was not willing to answer any questions Mom and Dad had about how she slept last night. They only asked her the questions because she usually has nightmares.

"Hey Amy, can you get your brother out of the house and off his phone please." Mom said.

"Ok, yeah sure." Amy replied.

"Thanks sweetheart!"

"Hey Zach, do you want to play soccer?" Amy asked.

"No!" I said.

"But Mom said you should stop playing video games and come play outside with me."

"Still not going.", I muttered.

"Young man! You will go outside with your sister and play soccer right this instant", Dad said forcefully.

"Jeez, why do you have to be so mean?"

"Because you make me mad, now do as you're told."
"Fine," I protested.
"Come on Zach lets go." Amy said.
"Yeah 'come on Zach lets go'" I said mockingly.
"I heard that Zach," mom said.
"Ugg".

I slammed the backyard door and went outside to play soccer with Amy. It was actually pretty fun. Amy thought she won on her own but I actually let her win.

The next day I just sat around all day in my PJs while Amy had to go out to chess club at 9:00 A.M. Sometimes I think that I'm the lucky one out of the two of us, but I wasn't that lucky when I ran into the thing in the woods.

5

That night I couldn't sleep with the thought of the thing almost killing me. It was about 3:40 A.M. when I got up out of bed to go see if I could find it again.

I got all dressed and ready to go find it. I was about to go back to my bedroom when the thought hit me, my door was locked when I shut it so going back to bed was a "No".

Now I regretted my choice to get out of bed. And I wasn't that desperate to wake up my parents or Amy so I just went outside unnoticed.

I was glad I came prepared, as I remembered how unrealistically big that thing was. I was shocked still with terror for at least a few moments until I remembered what I had packed was a flashlight, tiki-torch, a pitch fork, a pocket knife, some extra batteries for the flash light, and a lighter for the tiki-torch and all of that was stored in my backpack. I held the pitch fork in my hands. I had found the pitch fork in the old greenhouse we never cleaned out since we moved in

I took out the torch and lighter. At first it didn't light, but after the second try it worked. I was a little excited initially but once I left the proximity of the house I was terrified. I was about to go into a deep well of fog when I heard the house door shut. It was Amy.

"Zach what are you doing out here?" Amy asked in a whisper.

"What? How did you hear me?" I asked.

"It was pretty obvious when you shut your bedroom door. It was very loud."

"It was?"

"Yes, it was." Amy said.

"Good thing it didn't wake up Mom and Dad" I said.

"Yeah, good thing it didn't. By the way, why are you out here so late and why do you have a backpack, torch, and why are you holding a pitchfork?"

"Um...well...do you remember the night of my birthday?"

"Yeah." Amy said.

"Well, after you ran off back home something happened..."

"Well, what happened?"

"Well...um...nothing."

"What do you mean 'Nothing'?"

"Nothing...nothing happened", I stammered.

"Come on please tell me."

"You swear you won't tell Mom?"

"I swear.", Amy said.

"Good... When I came home with all the scratches that night it was from a...a...thing."

"What kind of thing?"

"A... a... werewolf... I think."

"Oh, Zach, you're funny.", Amy said laughing. "Now, this time, actually tell me why you're out here in the middle of the night with all that stuff?"

"Look Amy, I told you the truth. And I don't care whether you believe me or not. So you can follow me or go back to bed."

"Oh, you should care"

"Why?" I was getting mad.

"You know Mom and Dad's rule about not wielding sharp pointy objects, like, I don't know, a pitch fork!"

"You'd never tell. Plus, where's your proof?" I gloated.

"Oh, I don't know…. maybe on my voice recorder."

"You'd never!"

"Try me", Amy dared.

"Fine! I'll make you a deal. You don't tell Mom and Dad about this and I'll let you come with me. Deal?"

"Deal."

"Good." I said, a bit calmer now.

6

"So where are we going?", Amy asked.

"I don't exactly know."

"What...well did you at least search up how to kill a werewolf?"

"Ah... no?"

"So you're saying you dragged me out here in the middle of the night to go find a stupid were-wolf and you don't even know how to kill it? Am I correct?"

"Yeah, but-"

AWWWWOOOOO suddenly shattered the night's silence.

"What was that?" Amy asked.

"It's here."

"What's here?"

"You seriously don't remember that entire argument we just had?" I asked exasperated.

"Yes, I remember but I thought you were fibbing."

"Well, I wasn't!"

"Ok, well, if it's real and I am not saying it is... we can at least search up how to kill it."

"How?"

"I brought my phone", triumphed Amy.

"You brought that out here in the middle of the woods at 3:40 A.M?"

"Hey if I didn't, we might die trying to kill it."

"Fair point", I conceded. "Alright we can stop walking and search it up".

"Ok, it says here that you need something silver," Amy read. "It suggests a bullet."

"Well, we don't have a bullet or anything silver so we can't kill it.", I said.

"Wait a second. Is the pitchfork silver?"

"Well, we know that silver tarnishes so, is the pitch fork tarnished?" I asked.

"Yes".

"Ok, good. But the bad thing is that lots of other metals tarnish.", I said

"So, what you're saying is that we're probably going to die tonight."

"Yeah I guess so." I said with almost full belief.

"Well, that's just great.", Amy muttered.

"Yeah.", I sighed,

But just then we heard the shatter of glass into a million pieces.

"Run!" I shouted, before I even looked in the direction the noise came from.

"Why... ahhhhhh!", Amy screamed as I quickly grabbed her arm and ran towards the sound.

7

"Zach, let go...uhh!" Amy complained.

She pushed off and I went stumbling forward on to the ground with a thud.

"Amy, we have to keep going, someone might be in trouble."

"Well that someone might be us if we don't get out of here NOW!" Amy shouted.

She had a serious look on her face but the look in her eyes told me that she was more scared than serious.

"Uhh", I said as I got up off the ground. "Look Amy, if we stop here that werewolf will still be out there hunting and killing. Which is why we need to go instead of just standing here wasting our time arguing."

I then ran.

"Zach!" Amy yelled in disbelief but I was sprinting.

8

I ran out of the forest and could not find the werewolf.

"Hey, you left me back there all alone," Amy said as she ran up panting.

"Shhh!"

"Don't 'shhh' me now-"

Then I put my hand over her mouth but it didn't work cause all she did was keep talking and kept coming out in mumbles.

"Shhh! The thing,... the werewolf is hiding.", I said in a whisper.

Of course she tried to talk but I couldn't understand.

A rising, ear-splitting AWWWWOOOOO startled us. The werewolf was getting closer by the minute.

"We have to get moving.", I said in the quietest voice I could.

The next second we were running. I didn't know if the werewolf was behind us or not, but I decided not to look back.

We were panting when we got to where all the broken glass was. It was a salon named Felicio's but right now it looked like a total mess with broken windows, fire every-where and it looked like a disaster zone.

"Well Zach, your imaginary werewolf was here or it was just a natural cause like, I don't know, a lightning strike?" Amy chided.

"Amy, there were no lighting strikes while we were out in the woods."

"Yeah, well, it could have happened before we left the house".

"Ok, look Amy, I don't have time to argue with you. We have to investigate. Look around and see if the werewolf left any clues."

"Or we could just leave and go home to sleep in peace and let the grownups handle this."

"Amy, no grownups will believe us."

"Why, it's a perfectly believable story."

"Amy, it would be like trying to teach a cat how to speak. It's impossible."

"Fine!"

"Now I'm going to go check out what happened". It didn't seem like a bad idea at the time.

9

"Wow! this place is really messed up." I said.

"No kidding, it is messed up."

"Ok, we need to look for clues." I said.

There was a loud bang as something fell inside the salon. We both jumped. Then we heard a voice.

"Oh no! My salon. It's ruined. Oh, it's going to cost a fortune to repair all the damage!" a bald headed man said.

"Who is that!?" Amy asked.

"I think that's the owner of the store, Felicio." I replied.

"Well, let's go ask him!", Amy said.

We ran over to Felicio inside the store. It was getting harder to breathe from all the smoke.

"What are you kids doing here? Did you cause this?". Felicio asked.

"No. Are you the store owner-", I started to ask.

"Quiet! We'll talk once we get out of the building", Felicio said.

We made our way carefully out of the debris, coughing until we got out of the smoke.

"Ok fess up. Did you talk your dad or some college student into dressing up as that werewolf because if you did you owe me a lot of money."

"No.", I replied.

Felicio continued, "But I gotta hand it to you. The detail on that custom was good, not good but the best I've ever seen. I mean the attention to detail was great for a werewolf costume with its red and black plaid flannel shirt. It was baring its teeth. There was blood dripping down its muzzle all the way to the ground like it just came back from a fresh kill. The claws were freshly sharpened knives. It had tangled ragged fur dyed dark red. Its face was scared with bloodshot eyes that never seemed to stop staring directly through my soul..." He paused. "Sorry, got carried away. But in the end, you're in jail and I still keep my business."

"Um...Zach does that sound a lot like the werewolf on the cake?" Amy asked, shocked.

"Hold up." Felicio said. "We're not talking about that. We're talking about how you -"

"Amy, we got to go, like, now" I said, cutting off Felicio.

"Yep", she replied.

"Wait what?" Felicio said.

"Ok, sorry sir. Hope you have a good day. Bye!"

Amy yelled while I pulled her away. "Zach what are you doing?" Amy asked in astonishment.

"Amy, we had to leave. He was going to turn us in."

"Yeah, but aren't we just running straight to the thing? And plus, we don't even have any weapons besides that tiny little pitchfork." Amy asked.

"It is not a tiny pitchfork. I thought it would have been very useful... fine we'll wait until next Monday to capture and kill that thing. Ok? Plus, we need to rest."

"Good, And a shower. Whew, we both stink." said Amy.

"Ok, good but this week, we get ready."

"Let's go!".

We jogged all the way home, but this time not through the woods.

10

Today I woke Amy up to go and get ready. It was 5:00 A.M. and our parents were still sleeping so we had the house to ourselves.

"Alright Amy, wake up sleepyhead! We've got a werewolf to slay!" I whispered, pulling the covers off my sister.

Amy groaned and swatted at my hand. "Zach, it's 5:00 A.M.! Why are you waking me up so early?" Amy moaned

"Because today's the day we find a way to kill that thing," I declared, ignoring her complaints. "Remember, no capture, only kill!"

Amy grumbled but finally sat up. We tiptoed downstairs, careful not to wake Mom and Dad. We scarfed down breakfast bars and Amy managed to snag a banana before I could.

"Ok," Amy said, wiping her mouth with the back of her hand. "So, what's the plan? Are we just going to charge into the woods with your trusty pitchfork?"

"Plan A," I declared, grabbing a worn backpack, "we lure the beast away from town and somehow trap it."

"Trap it?" Amy scoffed. "With what? Shoeboxes and glitter?"

"Hey, glitter can be surprisingly effective," I mumbled, shoving a flashlight and some granola bars into the backpack.

Amy rolled her eyes but started rummaging through her own drawer. "Plan B?"

"We wing it," I said, trying to sound braver than I felt. "Seriously though, maybe we can find some information online or at the library. Silver bullets? Wolfsbane? Something besides a sparkly unicorn trap."

Amy snorted. "Great. Because every reputable website has a 'How to Slay a Werewolf' section."

"Maybe the library has some old books with some hints," I suggested. "Creepy old books hidden in the restricted section maybe?"

Amy raised an eyebrow. "You're getting awfully specific there, Zach. Have you been watching Goosebumps again?"

"Maybe," I admitted with a sheepish grin. "But hey, it's worth a shot, right?"

We rode our bicycles to the library.

After hours of fruitless crawling through Google searches and looking for books in the stacks, we decided to sneak into the library's restricted section.

The air hung heavy with the musty scent of old paper and forgotten knowledge. We tiptoed past towering shelves, the silence broken only by the creak of floorboards and our own nervous breaths.

Finally, tucked away in a dusty corner, we found a leather-bound book titled "Myths and Legends of the Unnatural." It looked promising. As we started skimming the pages, a loud cough echoed through the room.

"A-hem! Looking for something specific, young ones?"

We whirled around to find a stern-looking librarian glaring at us over her spectacles.

"Uh, no ma'am," I stammered, shoving the book back on the shelf. "Just browsing."

The librarian narrowed her eyes. "This section is restricted for a reason. Now shoo, before I have to call security."

We mumbled apologies and beat a hasty retreat, dejected. Just as we were about to leave the library empty-handed, Amy bumped into a display case, sending a book tumbling to the floor.

"Salem Witch Trials," she muttered, picking it up. "Wait a minute, Zach, didn't that creepy book talk about a witch who could deal with... supernatural creatures?"

As she read through the book, Amy said, "According to this creepy book, there's a witch in Salem, Massachusetts who can help us with werewolves."

A spark of hope ignited in my chest. "Maybe that's our ticket! We can't fight a monster with a flashlight and a granola bar, but a witch..."

"A witch sounds even crazier, Zach," Amy said, but a flicker of uncertainty shone in her eyes.

"Look," I said, "we're running out of options. It's either a grumpy librarian or a potentially helpful witch. Which sounds worse?"

Amy's eyes widened. "But Salem, Massachusetts? That's, like, hours away! And witches aren't real, Zach!"

"Maybe not," I said, "but this book seems pretty convincing. Besides, what other options do we have?"

Amy sighed. "Fine. But if this gets us grounded for the rest of summer, I'm blaming you."

We rode back home and spent the next hour convincing Mom and Dad to let us take a day trip to Salem. We fibbed about wanting to visit a historical museum, which technically wasn't a lie, since the witch would likely be very historical. Finally, after a lot of pleading and promising to be extra good, they agreed.

11

The drive to Salem felt like forever. Amy kept trying to scare me with stories of witches and curses, but I was too focused on our mission. We finally arrived in Salem, a quaint town filled with shops selling spooky souvenirs. We followed the directions in the book, which led us down narrow streets and finally to a creepy house at the edge of town.

A hunched figure with a pointy hat answered our knock. Her eyes, magnified by thick glasses, narrowed when she saw us.

"Children? What brings you to my doorstep?" her voice rasped.

We exchanged nervous glances.

"We, uh, need your help," I stammered.

The witch cackled, a sound that sent shivers down my spine. "Help, do you? And what kind of help could two youngsters possibly need from a crone like me?"

We explained about the werewolf, the fire at Felicio's salon, and our fear. The witch listened intently, a sly smile playing on her lips.

"So, you seek to slay a werewolf," she said finally. "A dangerous task, even for grown adults. But perhaps I can be of assistance."

12

The witch led us inside her house. It was filled with strange objects – bubbling cauldrons, dusty scrolls, and jars containing things I didn't even want to know about.

"There is a way," the witch said, her voice echoing in the cluttered room. "An ancient weapon, a silver sword, and a special poison that can weaken even the strongest werewolf."

Our hearts leaped with hope. But then the witch added, "Of course, nothing comes for free."

My stomach sank. "What do you want?" I asked warily.

The witch's smile widened. "A small token of gratitude. The werewolf's heart. Once the beast is slain, you will bring it to me."

Amy gasped. "But why would you want that?"

The witch's eyes gleamed. "To keep it safe, so no more werewolves roam free."

The witch cackled again, a sound that seemed to shake the very walls. She produced a beautiful silver sword that shimmered in the dim light and a vial filled with a glowing green liquid.

"This sword, forged under a full moon, can pierce even the toughest hide," she explained. "The poison will weaken the beast, making it vulnerable. But remember, children, use them wisely. The consequences of failure are dire. For if you fail, I collect your souls." She paused, looking into our eyes. "Do we have a deal?"

We looked at each other, fear battling with desperation. We knew the risks. If we failed, the witch would take our souls. But if we succeeded and didn't bring her the heart, who knew what she might do?

With a heavy heart, I said "Deal."

13

The drive back home was even more tense than the drive there. We knew what we had to do, but the weight of the deal with the witch pressed down on us. Silence hung heavy in the car, broken only by the hum of the road.

Reaching home, we snuck the sword and vial in through the basement door, hiding them in the boxes filled with toys, unused clothing and other junk. We knew nightfall, at the full moon, was when the beast would rise again. A knot of dread twisted in my stomach.

Dinner with Mom and Dad was a blur. We forced smiles and made small talk, all the while our minds were racing with a plan. We decided to set out on bikes searching for the werewolf, somewhere secluded where we could face it without endangering anyone else.

14

As dusk settled, casting long shadows across our back-yard, we snuck out the back door, the silver sword in my hand and the vial of poison hidden in Amy's backpack. We biked for miles, following a barely-there path deep into the woods.

The full moon cast an eerie glow through the trees as we biked deeper into the woods. The air grew colder, and the smell of wet fur became stronger.

"Zach, I don't like this," Amy whispered, her voice barely audible over the rustling leaves.

"Me neither," I admitted, my heart pounding a frantic rhythm against my ribs. "But we have to do this."

Suddenly, a deafening howl pierced the night, chilling me to the bone. We stopped our bikes, fear paralyzing us for a moment. My heart hammered against my ribs as the unmistakable scent of wet fur and decay filled the air.

"There!" Amy hissed, pointing towards a shadowy figure emerging from the undergrowth. "It's huge!"

The werewolf lumbered towards us, its eyes glowing like embers, fixed on Amy. Adrenaline surged through me, erasing the fear momentarily.

"Run!" I yelled, grabbing Amy's arm and pulling her towards our bikes. But she wouldn't budge, frozen in fear.

I was trembling in terror, but adrenaline surged through my veins. I picked up a rock and threw it to draw the creature's attention away from Amy. It roared and charged towards me.

15

I ran, my legs pumped, fueled by fear, drawing the were-wolf away from Amy and to me. I weaved through the trees, the werewolf hot on my heels.

I glanced back, seeing the creature right behind me. That's when I tripped and fell, banging my knee on a rock. The beast loomed over me, its breath washing over my face.

A scream tore from my throat, but before the werewolf could slice into me, Amy sprang out from behind it. She hurled the vial at the creature, it shattered and the glowing liquid splashed across its chest. It yelped in pain, smoke rising from where the poison made contact.

Seizing this opportunity, I scrambled to my feet and grabbed the silver sword. It felt surprisingly light in my hand, almost as if it were meant for me. With a deep breath, I lunged forward, plunging the blade into the werewolf's side.

The creature howled in agony, a sound that echoed through the night. The silver glowed white hot, burning a sizzling hole in the werewolf's flesh. It stumbled back, weakened and enraged.

The werewolf managed to charge, snapping its jaws and swiping its massive claws at me. I jumped back and used the trees for cover, dodging its attacks and striking back as best I could with the silver sword.

I was tired, unable to keep up my defenses for much longer. Then Amy yelled. "Zach! The heart! Aim for the heart! Stab it in the heart!"

Yes, the heart. The witch wanted the heart as a "prize" so it must be powerful. Maybe even the power that kept the werewolf alive.

With a final surge of strength, I screamed out and thrust the sword forward into the thing's chest, feeling it connect with a solid lump. The werewolf let out a deafening roar before collapsing in a heap, lifeless.

16

We stood there, panting and covered in sweat and dirt. The clearing was filled with an eerie silence, broken only by the chirping of crickets. Relief washed over me, tinged with a sense of dread at what we had done.

Using the sword, we cut out the heart, a pulsing, fleshy mass that felt unnaturally warm in my hand.

"Oh, gross!", Amy said.

"Shut up and help me".

Climbing back onto our bikes, we rode back home and crept into the house. We hid the silver sword back in the basement along with the heart and quietly made our way up the stairs to our bedrooms. We stopped for a moment and looked at each other.

"We can't tell anyone about this. Ever", I whispered.

Amy simply nodded and slipped into her room.

17

Morning arrived, casting a pale light on the events of the night before. We went about our day, pretending everything's Ok, but the werewolf hunt and the deal with the witch were on our minds.

A few days later, we had to go on a before-the-start-of-school field trip to, of course, Salem.

"I don't want to go. That witch scares me", Amy said.

"We have to go and give her the heart. If we don't, I think she gets our souls or something."

"Zach, we have to tell Mom and Dad".

"No! Never! We started this and we're going to finish it. I'm going to sneak into the basement, get the heart and shove it into my backpack. You keep Mom and Dad busy. I'll meet you out front and we can walk to the bus stop".

When the bus arrived, we climbed aboard, ignoring our friends, sitting glumly in the back row. The ride up felt long, longer than the last time.

"Is your backpack moving?" Amy asked.

"Yes, the thing's heart is still beating. It is really creeping me out".

"Keep it away from me!"

I felt a heavy weight in my stomach, that this was wrong. Giving this heart to the witch and her coven is a big mistake. But I didn't see any other choice.

The bus rumbled to a stop in front of an old 17th century building that looked even creepier in the morning light. "Ugh, Salem," Amy groaned, pulling her backpack closer.

"Come on," I muttered, my own stomach churning. "Just get the witch her prize and let's get out of here."

We cautiously approached the crooked doorway and knocked. The door creaked open, revealing the same hunched figure we'd met before.

"Well, well," the witch cackled, her voice like nails on a chalkboard. "Back so soon, children? Did you bring it?"

Amy and I exchanged a nervous glance. My hand reached for the backpack strap, where the heart thumped ominously.

"Uh, yeah," I stammered. "Here you go."

The witch extended a gnarled hand. "Excellent! Let's see it."

Just as I was about to hand her the heart, a mischievous glint sparked in Amy's eyes. "Wait a sec," she said. "We have a question."

The witch's eyes narrowed. "What is it, child? Don't waste my time."

"What exactly do you plan on doing with the heart?" Amy pressed.

The witch's smile widened, revealing a disturbing number of pointed teeth. "Why, my dears, with this heart as the key, I can finally cast the Great Howling Curse! A spell that will unleash an army of werewolves upon the world!"

My blood ran cold. We'd risked our lives to kill the were-wolf, only to hand its heart over to someone who planned on unleashing an entire pack of them!

"You lied to us!" I shouted, angry.

The witch cackled. "Naive children! You made a deal, and now you must uphold your end. Now hand it over!"

Amy and I locked eyes. There was no way we could let this happen. We'd already faced one werewolf. Facing a whole army was out of the question.

"Forget it!" Amy declared, shoving me back before I could react. "We're not giving you anything!"

The witch shrieked in rage, a cloud of green mist swirling around her. We scrambled back, hearts pounding like drums.

"You dare defy me?" she bellowed. "You'll pay dearly for this!"

18

But before the witch could unleash her wrath, we turned and bolted. We sprinted down the street, ignoring the witch's enraged screams echoing behind us. We didn't stop running until we were breathless and hidden within the woods on the other side of the old cemetery.

Collapsing against a stone wall, we panted heavily. Silence hung in the air, broken only by the chirping of birds.

"So much for keeping our deal," Amy said finally, a mixture of fear and relief in her voice.

"Yeah, thanks for that whole 'defy the witch' thing," I added with a playful nudge.

Amy punched my arm lightly. "Hey, someone had to do it! Besides, you were about to hand over the doomsday key!"

We sat there in silence for a moment, the weight of our decision settling in.

"What now?" I asked. "We can't just keep the heart forever."

Amy shook her head. "No, but maybe we can hide it. Somewhere safe, where no witch or coven will ever find it."

We cautiously made our way back to the school bus, climbed aboard and hid there until the rest of the students and teachers returned for the ride back home.

As we walked from the bus stop back home, we explored every nook and cranny of the woods around our house, searching for the perfect hiding place. We finally settled on a hollowed-out tree trunk deep within a hidden clearing, far from any trails or roads. We buried the heart beneath a thick layer of leaves and dirt, swearing a secret pact to never speak of it again.

As we entered our house, Mom and Dad greeted us with hugs and kisses.

"Did you two have a great time on the before-school-starts field trip? This is twice this summer you've been to Salem!", Mom asked.

I muttered, "Yeah, lots of fun".

"Well, let's get you dinner and to bed. Tomorrow's the first day of school!" Dad said.

"Don't mention school, dear. Have a heart!" Mom said.

Amy and I both looked at each other and groaned.

19

In the nearby clearing, where the heart is hidden in the hollow of a tree, it is peaceful and quiet. The snapping of twigs and crunching of leaves under foot disturbs the serenity, getting louder. Something is approaching. A hand reaches out to dig into the pile of leaves, branches and dirt. It pulls out the heart. The sound of leaves crunching and twigs snapping slowly recedes back into the woods.

9 798330 421473